THE MINE

BY MICHAEL YOWELL

SEVEREDPRESS

THE MINE

WWW.SEVEREDPRESS.COM

ISBN: 978-1-922861-95-5

1

"Do you ski?"

The unexpected question snapped Ellen back to full attention. She looked up from the doodling on her notepad. "Sorry?"

Nick Sanders was leaning forward in his chair, his chin resting atop interlaced fingers. He smiled and repeated himself. "Do you ski?"

Like most residents of Colorado, Ellen Hunter and her husband, John, did venture to the slopes to ski the winter snow. The ski resorts were packed with people going downhill skiing. So much so, that Ellen and John did not go unless they could get up there on a weekday, when fewer people were trying to share the mountain.

"Sure," she replied. "I mean, not as much as we used to. It's gotten too expensive, and way too crowded."

"That's true. What about cross-country skiing? Do you ever do that?"

"We do, once in a while," Ellen nodded. She and her husband still had their cross-country gear from when they were in college. They used to go on long ski trails all the time when they were younger.

"Because," said Nick, "I heard about a great trail up in Summit County. Goes all the way to the top of a peak. It's in the back roads, supposed to be very pretty, and practically no one knows about it."

"Nice." The reply was cordial, but Ellen was guarded. She wondered where he was going with this; skiing certainly wasn't one of the topics they were going to address in today's business meeting.

"Nancy says she'll go with me this weekend, and she wants you and your husband to join us."

Ellen tensed a bit. She and John had gotten together with the Sanderses before, and it was not unpleasant, but John always stated afterward that he did not like Nick at all. She feigned a smile. "Really?"

"Yeah," said Nick, "she loves spending time with you."

"Me too," Ellen admitted. "She's a nice lady."

Nick leaned in a little more. "So what do you say? Are you and John free Saturday? It's supposed to be good weather."

They were available. Ellen was not sure how John would react to the invitation, but the thought of trekking through the fresh air of the mountains sounded nice. "We have no plans, as far as I know," she said. "I'll ask John about it tonight."

Nick rocked back into his chair. "Good. It'll be great up there. Let me know, and I'll tell Nancy."

"All right."

That settled, Nick continued talking about his marketing ideas while Ellen jotted some of them down.

***

The drive home from work was tedious. Rush hour traffic was terrible in Denver. It took Ellen an hour to drive twenty miles. When she finally got home, she was even more inspired to get away to the mountains this weekend.

Ellen had an hour to make dinner. John worked retail, and today he was scheduled until seven. That was more than enough time to cook some chicken breasts with hot pepper paste, boil pasta for a seasoned side dish, and heat up a can of green beans as their vegetable serving.

When John came home, he looked fatigued. He kissed his wife and sat down with a long exhale. "What a day," the department manager sighed.

"Tough?"

"Just nothing but problem customers," he said. "Grumpy people all day long. Must be a full moon or something."

"Sorry, baby," said Ellen. "Well, now you're home and you can unwind." She plated their dinners and opened a bottle of wine.

"How was your day?" John inquired.

"Pretty good. Same ol' same ol'… better than your day, it sounds like."

He grinned and nodded. Ellen brought everything to the table and sat with him, and they ate.

After the meal, the couple refilled their wine glasses and migrated to the living room. There they would watch some TV from the couch. Ellen decided it was time to tell her husband about their weekend plans.

"What's the weather supposed to do this weekend?" she asked.

"I think it's supposed to be nice out."

"Even up in the mountains?"

John shrugged. "I don't know. Why?"

Ellen grinned innocently, pulling her silky brown hair away from her face. "I think we should go to the mountains Saturday."

John was not opposed to the idea. "We could. What do you want to do up there?"

"How long has it been since we went cross-country skiing?"

"Oh wow, it's been a while," John reflected. "That would be fun, though."

Ellen fidgeted in her seat. "We'd be going with another couple. They know where a fantastic trail is."

"Really? Who?"

She squinted while delivering her reply. "Nick and Nancy."

He grimaced. "Jesus, honey…."

"He says it's an awesome trail, very pretty."

"I'm sure it is," said John, "but Nick… he's just so… arrogant, so annoying…"

"He's also my boss."

"He's a dick," John declared, summing up his assessment of Nick. He hated listening to Nick brag about his business, his money, and his excursions. In fact, John was a little jealous.

"Oh come on," said Ellen. "He actually likes you. He wants us both to go."

"I'm surprised he didn't plan a trip for just the two of you."

Ellen raised an eyebrow. "And just what is *that* supposed to mean?"

"He seems *very* fond of you."

"What?"

"I've seen it in the way he looks at you. More than once."

Ellen wasn't stupid; she too had picked up on The Vibe occasionally. She knew her husband was right, but Nick Sanders posed no threat. Not once had he ever outwardly said or done anything inappropriate.

"He's harmless," stated Ellen. "And," she reiterated, "he's my boss."

"Yeah? How much would he pay you to—"

"Watch it." At this point they were just bantering playfully. They chuckled at each other, and Ellen recognized John's guard was dissolving. "So what do you say? Can we go skiing Saturday?"

John shrugged. A day in the mountains would be pleasant, regardless of the company. And besides, it seemed like something Ellen really wanted to do.

"Yeah, I suppose we could," he surrendered.

Ellen smiled. "Good." She gave him a kiss. "It'll be a fun day, you'll see."

2

The weekend was here. John and Ellen had packed up their Ford Explorer and were driving to the coffee house where everyone had agreed to meet. Ellen glanced over at John, and she noticed the moping look on his face.

"Cheer up," she said. "This'll be fun."

John forced a grin. "I know, I know. I just have to focus on the beautiful scenery instead of the company."

"John!"

He chuckled. "Sorry, baby. Don't worry, I'll behave."

She looked at him suspiciously.

"I will," he promised. "This'll be fun."

"This'll be fun," she repeated.

Ellen continued driving through the moderate Saturday-morning traffic. There were cars packed with families doing whatever activities were planned for today. A few delivery trucks were out. A good number of vehicles had downhill-skiing gear secured on top, indicating they were heading up the mountains to the crowded ski resorts.

When Ellen arrived at the coffee house, she parked the Explorer and turned the motor off.

"Looks like we beat them here," she said after a quick glance around the parking lot.

John got out of the Explorer and moved to the back to retrieve his skis. While they were waiting, he figured he would wax his skis. He grabbed the stick of glide wax and started applying it to the underside of his skis at the tips and tails to keep snow from sticking to them.

Seeing this, Ellen decided to wax her skis as well. "Good idea, babe. We won't have to do it when we get up there."

Minutes later, a black Cadillac Escalade pulled up next to them. Nick and his wife stepped out to greet their companions.

"Hi," said Ellen.

"Hello!" Nick's wife, Nancy, came over to give Ellen a light hug. "How are you?"

"I'm good, Nancy. How've you been?"

"Can't complain. Oh my God, it's been so long! It's good to see you again!"

Ellen smiled; Nancy had truly missed her. "You too."

"Hello, John," said Nick, extending his hand.

John shook it. "Hey, Nick. How's it going?" He couldn't help but notice that Nick had his dirty-blond hair fixed up with gel. *Dummy*, he thought, *you're gonna be wearing a hat today*. He almost rolled his eyes.

"Good, good," Nick said. "Looks like a beautiful day for some skiing, huh?"

It really was. The sky was a dome of rich blue, made warm by the sun. There were hardly any clouds floating in the air.

"It sure is," John admitted. "Gonna be nice."

Nick nodded. "So. You still working retail?"

"Yep. Department manager."

Nick's face could not hide his judgmentalism. "Really?"

"Yeah—I make good pay. And I get great health coverage for Ellen and me, which we both need."

"Ellen tells me you're pretty handy," Nick remarked. "You should just go into business for yourself."

"I would, if you could ever offer health coverage to your employees and their spouses."

Nick's hands flew up. "Hey, that's a little below the belt," he chuckled. "Do you have any idea how much it costs for a small business like mine to offer benefits?"

"I can imagine," said John. He finished waxing his skis.

"So where are we heading?" Ellen inquired.

Nick turned to his office assistant. "We're gonna go up I-70. Then, just before Copper Mountain, we'll turn off to the frontage road. After that it's about another half an hour of back roads to the mountain trail."

"Our neighbors told us about it," Nancy added. "They said that from the top, you can see a hundred miles around."

"Sounds good," said Ellen.

Nick's eyes did a quick and subtle scan of Ellen. He could not help but notice that even in her loose ski pants, her curvy figure showed.

John caught the glance. He clacked his skis together. The sharp sound jolted Nick, making him jump just the tiniest bit. The reaction made John want to chuckle. His suspicion of Nick's attraction to Ellen seemingly confirmed, John would keep his eye on Nick.

"So," said Nick, "do we want to just take one car?"

Ellen faced her husband. "I don't know. Do you wanna?"

John shrugged. "I'm cool with taking two cars," he stated. "Especially with all our gear."

"Nonsense," said Nancy, shaking her head and making her shoulder-length black hair swish. "There's plenty of room in the Escalade. The skis will all fit on top, and everything else can lie in the back."

"Plus, we'd save on gas," Ellen noted.

John realized that the group consensus was to take one vehicle. It wouldn't be terrible, he supposed. Besides, it would give Nancy plenty of time to chat with Ellen.

"Okay," he said. "Carpool it is."

***

Nick drove his luxury SUV up the winding highway ascending into the Rocky Mountains. John was sure that Nick would drive him crazy talking about himself the whole time. To John's surprise, however, Nick's conversations were interesting and engaging. Even the music playlist—consisting of rock bands such as Lynyrd Skynyrd, AC/DC, and Led Zeppelin—was one that John enjoyed hearing.

The travelers continued up I-70. As they gained altitude, their ears popped now and then. After two hours of driving, they were at 10,000 feet.

Nick exited the highway just before reaching the base of Copper Mountain, one of the more popular downhill-skiing resorts. Taking a frontage road away from the resort and eventually away from the highway, they drove up the side of a mountain for another half hour.

Finally, they arrived at the end of the road. At an altitude of 11,000 feet, the spot was very isolated. There were no other vehicles that had come there. Nick's group would have the whole trail to themselves.

Everybody got out of the Escalade and walked around, stretching. Nick started bringing the skis down from the roof rack.

John looked around. He could barely see the trailhead at the edge of the woods. It was practically hidden.

"What a gorgeous day," said Ellen, admiring their surroundings under the deep-blue sky. She kissed John. "This is gonna be so nice!"

Nick sucked in a deep breath of mountain air. "What do you think?" he asked his companions. "Is this perfect, or what?"

"It looks great," said John, studying the wooded slope ahead of them.

Eager to go on their journey into the wilderness, the group bundled up and put their gear on. They clamped their boots into the skinny skis, followed Nick into the trees, and started striding up the mountain.

3

John was finally glad he'd agreed to come. Trekking up the mountainside was invigorating. The crisp air, the heavy scent of pine, the sights of lush green and glistening white, and exciting terrain through which to ski—he loved it. Plus, it was great exercise.

The group spent hours on the trail getting to higher elevation. As they ascended, they passed remnants of what used to be shacks long ago.

"Who do you think lived here?" Nancy wondered.

"Old miners, I'm sure," said Nick. "There was a lot of silver mining around here in the 1880s. And then a gold rush after that."

John was slightly impressed. "Wow, you know some local history."

"I'm a Colorado native," Nick shrugged. "We learn these things."

Being a state native himself, John nodded. He remembered learning about Colorado mining when he was a kid. Hearing about it in elementary school had made him dig around in his back yard, hoping to unearth nuggets of gold. One time he'd found a rock covered with shiny gold, and he'd excitedly run inside to show his parents. He was disappointed when his father told him that the mineral was pyrite—also referred to as fool's gold—and not gold. John kept it in his room anyway, because it looked cool.

They went higher, and the slope grew a little steeper. The trail addressed that by weaving across the steep areas. Not only did that make skiing up the mountain easier, but it would make for a safer, slower glide when coming back down.

Nick led the way up the trail, followed by his wife, then Ellen, and John brought up the rear. Up here, the passage was only wide enough to travel single file.

Ellen noted the back of Nancy's haircut; that shiny black hair was cut perfectly, undoubtedly at her usual salon by her usual stylist. Nancy always looked good, at least each time Ellen had seen her. She had a great complexion, did her makeup very well, and her hairstyle was always pretty. It was obvious that Nancy was used to spending time on herself and her appearance. But, unlike most women with her financial status, Nancy was sweet and friendly to everyone.

"So, what's it like working for my husband?" Nancy asked, looking over her shoulder to Ellen. "He'd better not be working you too hard."

"Nah," said Ellen. "He's a pretty good boss."

He'd better be, thought John. He glanced ahead at Nick to see what reaction he might have.

Nick looked back at the group and smiled. "Of *course* I'm a good boss. I'm not a monster, you know."

Nancy toyed with him. "You have your moments."

His eyebrows rose. "Oh? I guess we'll find out when we get home." He then growled at her like what he thought a monster would sound like.

John and Ellen chuckled, entertained by the exchange. It reminded them of their own playful bantering.

"Besides," Nick added, "Ellen's a terrific employee. She's never late, she takes care of everything, and she makes sure the computer's always trouble free. She's awesome."

John nodded. "That she is."

"Oh stop," Ellen said sarcastically to both of them. "You *know* how I hate flattery."

John smirked and rolled his eyes. "Yeah right, like I hate steak."

The group laughed together.

They continued traversing up the mountain. Stopping occasionally for drinking and snacking, or to pee, they eventually made it to the tree line, where the air was too thin for trees to grow. They were just about at the top of the peak.

"Wow," said Ellen, taking in the view of the Rocky Mountains all around them. She brought out her phone, noticing that she had no signal. She didn't care about that; she was after the camera. Ellen opened the camera app and took some panoramic pictures.

"A perfect place to stop," said Nancy.

They enjoyed the moment. They had made it to the top of the trail. And it was worth it; the sights from 12,000 feet were breathtaking.

Nick pulled out a small Cohiba cigar and lit it with his WindBlaze lighter.

Nancy rolled her eyes. "Ugh. You and your cigars."

"What?" Nick said defensively. "I don't smoke 'em that often. And you know I always have one when I'm in the mountains. It's my tradition."

She chuckled. "That's true."

Nick turned to John and pulled another Cohiba from his parka's inside pocket. "Have a stogie?"

"No, thanks," said John.

Nick wiggled it in the air. "Are you sure? It's Cuban."

John deliberated for a moment. He had smoked cigars before, albeit very rarely. But if there was an occasion suitable for a cigar, this was one of them.

"On second thought," John said, reaching over, "I think I'll take you up on that."

Nick smiled and handed the cigar and his torch lighter to his comrade.

John lit it and puffed until it was burning strong. "Thanks," he said, giving the lighter back.

The two men smoked their cigars while admiring the magnificent view from the top of the snowy peaks.

4

The snowstorm came suddenly.

Rolling in behind the resting skiers, blankets of dark clouds were coming fast. They quickly blocked out the afternoon sun.

"Whoa," said John, noticing the oncoming cloud bank, "look at this."

Nick turned to see the surprise storm front. "Holy shit."

In minutes, the storm swooped in. Blasts of icy wind pushed down, bringing a flurry of heavy snow with them.

The chill gripped John's body. Since the group was above the tree line, there was nothing to shield them from the wind and snow. The numbing cold of the sudden change in weather made John put his gloves and stocking cap back on.

Ellen tightened her scarf. Then she gave her husband a puzzled look. Colorado winters were unpredictable, but she would have never expected a change as abrupt and drastic as this.

"John?" she said concernedly. "What's happening?"

"No idea," he admitted. "I didn't check the weather update for this weekend."

"What? Why not?"

"I just assumed one of you did."

Nick shrugged. "We didn't check it either. Not recently, anyway. But earlier in the week, they'd projected a clear forecast."

"I can't believe none of us checked the weather forecast today!" Nancy said incredulously. "I feel so stupid!"

"We'd better head back," Ellen said, shivering. "This looks really bad." The dense storm front had all but swallowed the sun now, and the snow was falling thick and heavy.

"Yeah, that would be wise," added Nick. He and Nancy were also shuddering from the arctic fury of the sudden storm. *Crazy*, he thought. *Half an hour ago, it was such a lovely day.*

John adjusted his knitted cap. "I don't know," he muttered, examining their surroundings. The storm was growing worse by the second, threatening to bury the group in snow before long. The four of them would not last long if it got much worse. "This looks like it could be a blizzard," John stated. "If it turns into a whiteout, we might not make it all the way back down the mountain."

"We don't have any choice," said Ellen.

John detected a touch of panic in her voice. He struggled to provide a comforting reply, but he realized she was right; their only chance was to try to get down the mountain before freezing to death.

"Hey!" exclaimed Nick. "Look over there!"

All eyes followed his finger in search of what he had seen. Nancy now saw it too. "Right over that hill," she said, pointing a hundred yards to the north. There, at the top of a ridge, was a faint pillar of smoke. Its source, however, was hidden from view.

"It must be a shelter of some sort," John deduced. "Let's check it out! We can hunker down there until the storm blows over." Hearing this, the group continued uphill to the crest of the ridge.

Upon reaching the top, they saw a little cabin and a woodshed nestled away in a small, shallow valley. Smiling, John motioned for the others to follow him down the side of the valley. He leaned forward and let his skis accelerate down the hill, carrying him the rest of the way.

Smoke was rising from the cabin's chimney. The sight of this bolstered the group's yearning for shelter and warmth. Upon reaching the front door, the visitors alleviated themselves of their ski equipment. John then knocked on the door.

There was no response.

He knocked again, harder. "Hello! Is there anybody in there?"

The icy wind began to blow harder, magnifying the cold. "Hey John," whined Nick. "Just open it!"

John was hesitant. "What would the owner think if he came back to find that we had just let ourselves in? He might shoot us for breaking and entering."

"If he's not already inside, he's not coming back any time soon." Nick nodded toward a pair of half-buried snowshoes. "He wasn't going anywhere today without these."

The group leaned closer to examine the snowshoes, noting the name EDWIN JOHNSON boldly carved into each one of them.

John tried the door handle. It was unlocked. Shrugging to Ellen, he opened the door.

"Hello!" he called out once more. "Anybody home?"

Again there was no reply.

It seemed that nobody was home to answer. John entered the cabin and the others pressed behind him.

5

Once inside, John was struck by sudden blindness. There were no windows in the cabin, and his eyes were used to the brightness of the whiteout outside. As his sight adjusted to the darker environment, he took in the rustic scene before him.

The kitchen he was standing in was equipped with a wood-burning stove, pots and pans, and a supply of canned goods. Beyond the kitchen was a large room that contained a hand-made table, matching chairs, a faded couch, and a moss-rock fireplace. There was a fire burning, obviously the source of the smoke that led them there.

Strange, thought Nick, who came in behind John. *There's no sign of the owner anywhere, yet a fire is burning in the fireplace.*

John too was curious about this. Whoever had started this fire was nowhere to be seen now. *Weird.*

John turned toward the kitchen again, seeing the women shake themselves of snow. Nick brushed past him and went outside to bring the ski equipment in. But despite the others being in his view, John felt another presence. He had the uneasy feeling that somebody else was in the cabin with them… watching them.

He turned back around to find himself facing a mounted deer head. Its black-glass eyes stared back at him, and he could see his dim reflection in them.

John chuckled to himself, then sat down to warm up by the fire. The others joined him, slowly regaining feeling in their faces and fingers. John scanned the room repeatedly, seeing oil paintings and the deer head on the otherwise barren walls that were built from logs and cement. There were only two doorways in the main room. One to the kitchen through which they had entered, and one to a closet on the back wall. The closet door was closed. Yet John still couldn't shake the feeling that they were being watched.

***

Outside, the wind howled like a banshee. Snow began to blow around wildly and heavily. Visibility was worsening. A drift began to cover the back side of the cabin, and had almost claimed the back of the adjacent woodshed.

But the snow had not yet completely covered the body behind the woodshed.

***

An hour passed. The storm was still raging, and the snowfall was building up. The group was likely to be snowbound for quite a while. Maybe overnight. And there was no signal for their phones, so they couldn't call for help; they would just have to ride it out.

"I'm hungry," Nick declared. "Do we have any snacks left?"

Nancy shook her head.

"Any trail mix? Protein bars?"

"No, honey. We already ate them all."

"No more jerky?"

"No."

Talk of food was making John hungry as well. "We're gonna need to eat something, eventually. Especially if the blizzard goes on through the night."

"There's food in that kitchen," Ellen remarked.

"That belongs to whoever lives here," said Nancy. "That Edwin Johnson guy."

"Shit, I'll pay for it," Nick chortled. "I'll leave him more than enough cash to pay for what we eat of his."

Nancy was satisfied with that. "Then all right."

The group went to the small kitchen. They perused some of the canned goods, finding some cans of vegetable soup that looked tasty. There were pans to heat it in, and they could melt some of the snow from outside for their water. All they needed now was to fire up the wood-burning stove.

There was a small supply of kindling and paper in a cardboard box next to the stove, along with a box of stick matches and a few pieces of firewood to keep the fire going.

Each couple prepared their own pot of soup to share. They brought the food to the living area, sat down, and began to eat together. They watched the flames dance in the fireplace while they ate. John took note of the small bundle of firewood stacked next to the fireplace.

"I wonder who this Edwin Johnson is," pondered Ellen, taking another spoonful of soup.

"Probably some old hippie hermit," Nancy replied. "I wonder why he's not here."

"He was probably going down as we were coming up," mused John, chuckling. "Maybe he's at the bottom of the mountain seeking shelter in your car." The others pictured this and laughed with him.

"I'd rather be stuck in here during a snowstorm than stuck together inside a vehicle," giggled Nancy.

Ellen suddenly stopped laughing. "Quiet! Did you hear that?"

"What?" asked John, still smiling.

"Listen," she said, as the others quieted down. A faint creaking noise was heard.

"It's coming from that closet," said Nick. "Aw, it's probably just a mouse making noise."

Nancy tensed. "A mouse? I hate mice!"

"Don't worry, honey," joked Nick, "he won't eat very much of you."

"That's not funny."

It was a little funny, John acknowledged.

Again the noise, and John raised an eyebrow to Nick. "That's not a mouse," said John. "That sounded more like a door hinge."

Everyone stared at each other with unease, wondering if the cabin's owner was watching them from inside the closet.

"Hello?" Nancy called to the closet. "We're sorry we came in, but we needed shelter from the storm. We're friendly."

There was no response.

John slowly approached the closet door, and Nick followed. Nancy and Ellen tensed on the couch as the men prepared to open the door. John grabbed the doorknob, looked at Nick, and they nodded to each other. John yanked the closet door open.

Nothing was there except for clothing and blankets.

"Okay," Ellen exhaled, "I feel like a ninny."

"You shouldn't," said John. "Something was in here. We all heard it. But where is it? It couldn't have just disappeared."

Nick agreed. He bent down and started exploring the closet. He brushed aside musty blankets in an attempt to get a clear view of the back wall and floor. Suddenly he recoiled as he felt something sharp grab his hand. His reaction made the others jump as well.

"It's okay," he informed them, "I just caught my hand on the corner of a hinge."

"What, like a door?" asked John while Nick uncovered the floor.

"Yeah," he eventually replied when he'd cleared the floor to expose the entire door. It was a square piece of plywood with two hinges and a bolt latch that was not engaged. "Looks like a trapdoor to somewhere below."

"There's nothing below here but the ground," said John.

"Then maybe it goes underground."

Nancy suddenly felt apprehensive of what might be on the other side of that trapdoor. A dark feeling shot through her. "I don't think we should be in here," she whimpered. "We should get out of here. This just doesn't *feel* right."

"And just where do you propose we go?" snapped Nick. "Just mosey on out into this blizzard and hope we make it down the mountain before we freeze to death? Would that *feel* more right to you?"

"Hey, hey, guys," interrupted John. "This is a little freaky having to be here, for all of us… but let's stay cool. We're probably going to be stuck here overnight, or at least until the storm blows over."

Nancy couldn't understand why she was so afraid. "We shouldn't be here," she said, her eyes fixed on the trapdoor in the closet.

"It's okay," Ellen assured. "If the owner was here, I'm sure he would have no problem with letting us stay. He certainly wouldn't want us to freeze to death outside."

They all agreed. Nick glanced at his wife apologetically. "I'm sorry, honey." He then noticed that she looked cold. "How's the fire going?" he probed.

Nancy looked over her shoulder, seeing that the fire was almost out. She walked over to the fireplace and placed several more logs on top of the embers.

John studied the diminishing stack of wood and raised an eyebrow. "I don't know if that's gonna be enough firewood to get us through the night. Is there any more wood left in the kitchen?"

"Just some kindling for the stove," replied Ellen. "But wasn't there a little woodshed outside?"

"Yeah," said Nick, reaching for his boots. "I'll run out and bring back some more logs. Hopefully I'll find enough wood to keep the fire going all night. If we're gonna be stuck here for the night, I should go now anyway. The snow will just get deeper the longer we wait."

"You're right about that," John said. He watched Nick don his parka to get them firewood, and he realized that Nick was a pretty good guy after all.

Nick zipped up his parka and pushed the front door open, plowing through the accumulating snow outside.

6

Visibility was increasingly bad now, as the snow was pummeling the mountain. Nick shook his head in disbelief that he was stuck in this predicament, then continued toward the woodshed. Once there, however, he discovered that the door was secured with a padlock. *Damn*, he thought. *Now what do I do?* They had not noticed any keys inside, and he didn't really feel like going back to search for one. Instead, he decided to go around the woodshed to see if there was a window in back that he could enter through. Rounding the corner, he was pleased to find that there was indeed a large window on the back side, big enough for him to easily get in and out of.

Nick then tripped over something and landed face first into the fresh powder.

"Goddammit," he said. He rolled over to see what he had tripped on. It looked like a fallen tree limb, hidden under a thin layer of white. He kicked out at it in anger. As his foot struck it, however, the action jarred enough snow to reveal a pale human hand at the end of it. Nick realized there was a body there.

"Jesus!"

Panting in shock, he began to uncover the body. *This must be the owner of the cabin*, he surmised. *But why the hell was he out here?*

The snow and ice had been accumulating long enough to all but bury the victim. Looking upward at the blizzard, Nick decided to return his attention to the task at hand. He moved on, trudging through the snowdrift toward the window.

The window's glass was just a single fixed pane, so Nick easily shattered the glass with his elbow. Clearing the shards from the window frame, he wriggled inside. He then began looking for kindling and logs for the fireplace.

His eyes adjusted to the dark, and he found exactly what he was looking for. As he approached the neat stack of firewood, he heard something crack beneath him. He froze and looked down to discover that he was standing on a weathered piece of plywood that was bending under his weight. Slowly, he stepped off the plywood and moved it aside.

Where the plywood had been was now a black hole, only the railroad ties of the surface frame visible. *Holy shit*, he thought, *I almost fell into a mineshaft!* He drew a deep breath and went around it to get to the firewood.

Is that blood?

It looked like blood, or some other dark liquid, had been spilled on the earthen floor. A trail of it led to the locked door. *Whatever*, he thought, placing his focus on getting the wood.

He pulled all of the logs from the stack and tossed them out the window. Then, after climbing back outside, he wrapped his arms around half a dozen logs and carried them back to the cabin.

"Hey, John," Nick said when he entered the living area. "Come outside and help me bring in the wood, will ya?"

John jumped to his feet. "You bet." He then threw his parka on and followed Nick back outside.

"Man," said Nick while they walked against the wet, icy snowfall, "you won't believe what I found behind the shed."

"Yeah? What's that?"

"I—um—think it's the owner."

John's heart skipped a beat. "You mean he's dead?"

"Yeah. Come on."

Nick brought John around the woodshed, and John's eyes fell on the hand, arm, and shoulder of the partially-buried man.

"Oh my God," said John. This was the first time he'd actually been in the presence of a dead body. "What do you think happened?"

"No idea."

"Jesus…."

Nick turned to the pile of logs. "Come on, let's hurry up and get this all inside!"

After several trips back and forth, Nick and John had brought enough firewood to last overnight. Once they had taken their parkas off, they informed the women of the body Nick had found. The women gasped, shocked by the news, instinctively covering their mouths with their hands.

Ellen was shocked, but also intrigued. "Did you dig the body out to see what happened to him?"

"No," admitted Nick, "I didn't really feel like messing with it. Plus, the snow was falling too hard."

"Man," wheezed Nancy, with fear in her voice. "This just keeps getting better and better!"

"Relax, honey," Nick reassured her. "We'll get out of this just fine. You'll see." He draped an arm around her and pulled her snugly against him.

Soon the fire was roaring again, and the cabin was bright and toasty. The group had resorted to playing charades to pass the time.

Suddenly a creaking sound emanated from within the closet again. Then some faint scratching.

"Did you hear that?" John asked.

The others nodded. Ellen's eyes were big with concern.

John's curiosity won over. "That's it; let's find out what the hell that is."

The women looked at each other with hesitation in their eyes as the men again approached the closet door. This time Nick grabbed the handle, and he nodded to the others as he wrenched the door open.

Again, nothing was there.

"The sounds were definitely coming from here, probably beneath the trapdoor," whispered Nick. "Do we open it?"

"We'd better," John replied. "I'd rather find out what's causing that noise now than when we're asleep tonight."

"It's probably an access door to a mining tunnel or something," Nick offered. "I found an old mineshaft inside the woodshed. This whole valley's probably an old abandoned mine."

"Could be."

Nick turned to his wife. "Bring me that flashlight, will you, hon?"

Nancy picked up the flashlight and tentatively approached the closet. She stopped several feet away and tossed the flashlight to her husband.

Nick chuckled at his wife's skittishness, then turned back to John. "You open the door, and I'll hold the light."

John reached for the crease in the floor and slowly pulled the trapdoor open. Nick was using the flashlight for both a light source and a potential club, nervously awaiting whatever had made those noises. He expected something to leap out at him from the darkness, but nothing did.

"Looks like there's nothing here," Nick reported to his wife behind him.

"Check it out," said John, taking the flashlight from Nick. "There's a ladder here that looks like it goes down to a cellar. Maybe there's more food and supplies down there."

Nick smiled. "Nice."

"I'm gonna check it out." John positioned himself over the opening, holding the flashlight in one hand, and began his descent.

"Be careful," said Ellen while John disappeared through the closet trapdoor.

7

He descended the ladder, the flashlight beam scanning the new environment. The floor and walls were nothing but excavated earth and rock. The chamber was the beginning of a long stretch of tunnel, but the light from the flashlight could not help John determine the length of it. This was clearly part of a mine; there were railroad ties every ten feet bracing the rock in the tunnel.

He aimed the light back into the chamber he was in, studying his surroundings. There was a large wooden chest on the ground in front of him. He moved forward to better inspect it.

The chest was made of heavy oak, and was extremely weathered. *Lord knows how long this thing has been down here*, John wondered. Tarnished brass hinges and locks held the oak chest secure. If there was anything worth seeing in here, he would have to break into it. He turned his attention back to the long tunnel and began to wonder where it led to.

"How are you doing down there?" Nick queried, breaking John's focus on the tunnel. "See any noise-makers?"

Whatever had made the scratching noises did not seem to be anywhere in the chamber. John had looked around and seen nothing. He had failed to notice a crevice, however, in the dark behind the ladder next to him.

Inside the crevice, a pair of eyes studied him intently.

"Not much down here," he replied. "Just a big wooden chest and a long, dark tunnel."

"A tunnel?" he heard Ellen ask.

"Sure," said Nick. "I told you, this whole valley's probably a big mine. Probably from the silver and gold rushes of the late nineteenth century. Heck, maybe what we heard was caused by air blowing through the mine and up against the trapdoor."

"Wanna come down?" asked John.

"Yeah." Nick came down the ladder. Once on the ground below, he took the flashlight back from John and surveyed the chamber. "Wow," he mumbled, "would you look at this."

"I doubt if there's anything good in that chest," offered John, "but if you want to see what's inside, be my guest."

"Naw, probably just some old mining gear or something."

"Hmm," pondered John. "If we had mining gear, we could go check out the tunnel there and see where it leads to."

Nick raised a boyish eyebrow. "Do you want to?"

"Heck yeah. But is it safe to?"

Nick studied the railroad ties. "The bracings still look pretty stable to me. If it starts to look too dangerous, we can just turn back and join the women."

John committed himself to this expedition. "All right, let's do it. First, let's get this upstairs and find a way to open this thing."

The two men climbed the ladder with the heavy chest elevated above them, emerging from the closet and pushing the chest into the living area.

"Ooh," said Ellen, "what's this?"

"Buried treasure, me hearty," John said with a bad pirate voice.

Nick chuckled. "Hopefully there's some mining gear inside. There's a long tunnel down there leading somewhere."

Nancy was concerned. "That doesn't sound like a good idea."

"We'll be perfectly safe," said Nick. "And if it looks dangerous, we'll get out of there and come back."

Ellen didn't say a word. She knew her husband was the type of man who acted on instinct, and could not be swayed once he got an idea in his head. She figured Nick was the same way.

"Here," said Nick, pulling out a small hand axe from his backpack. "This ought to open that up fairly easily."

"Wait a minute," Ellen protested. "You can't just break into it. That's someone else's property."

Nick shrugged. "I'll leave him a little more cash for any damage."

John smiled. "All right, then," he said, smiling while taking the axe from his cohort. "Let's just see what's inside here."

He turned the axe around and struck the lock several times with the blunt end, but to no avail. The lock held secure. John grunted, frowning down at the stubborn lock. Then he turned the axe back around and started chopping at the wood that the lock was bolted onto. The aged wood quickly gave, and the lock fell harmlessly to the floor as the oak was hacked.

John raised the lid off the chest, and the others drew closer to see what was inside. There was a ragged book, bound in leather, and several newspaper articles. There were also some odd carved-rock idols, most of which were decorated with some sort of scratchy writing. John pulled those things out and laid them on the floor behind him, then returned to the chest to see what other items lay below. His eyes widened.

He pulled out half a dozen sticks of what appeared to be dynamite. The rest of the group stepped back. "Is that what I think it is?" asked Ellen. John examined one of the sticks, then turned to his wife and nodded.

"Better put those somewhere where they won't be disturbed," Nick suggested. "Maybe we should put them out in the snow. God only knows how old and unstable they are."

"Fuses look good," John noted. "But we probably shouldn't mess around with these." Ever so gently, he gathered the explosives and cradled them in his hands. "Get the door for me, will ya?"

Nick marched to the door and opened it. John took several steps into the deepening snow and placed the dynamite harmlessly there. Then the men went back inside to continue exploring the chest.

"Hey look!" said John. He reached in, pulled out a bundle of mining gear, and tossed it to Nick. "This is what we were looking for."

There were two pairs of mining boots, a small pickaxe, and miner's helmets with headlamps attached above the brim. Nick examined the gear, then took his ski shoes off to see if any of the mining boots fit. They did. John donned the other pair of boots and smiled at the fit, although they were still pretty tight around his feet. They then tested the helmet's headlamps. The men were pleased to see that the lamps boasted full, bright beams of light when switched on.

"Okay," said John. "I think we're ready." Nick nodded, and the two went through the trapdoor and back down the ladder.

"Wow," Nick said as his lamp illuminated the chamber. "This is gonna be cool." He aimed his helmet at the tunnel and held the light on it. "You want to go first?"

"Sure," John replied. "I'm up for the challenge." Cautiously, he headed into the tunnel. He moved his headlamp all over in order to be aware of his surroundings every step of the way. He would keep a sharp eye out for any signs of loose rock above him. Nick followed close behind.

"Hey, what makes you think these support beams are stable?" John asked. "They look to be a hundred years old."

"I think they're still fine. They do look pretty old, but they're not rotted. And I don't think it's been very long since somebody's been down here checking them."

"What makes you think that?"

"Well," said Nick, "these lights that were in the chest seem to have some full batteries. Whoever used them must've put the batteries in there pretty recently."

"That's true," John realized. "I wonder what the owner of this gear uses it for."

"Beats me," Nick shrugged. "But I imagine we'll find out if we keep going."

The two men slowly continued down the tunnel.

8

Back in the cabin above, the women were curious. They decided to examine the contents from the chest. Ellen reached for the rock carvings in particular. She thought they were quite intriguing upon first seeing them, although the men had all but ignored them during their earlier exploration of the chest. Now she could study them herself.

"Aren't these interesting?" she said, holding up one of the carved figures.

"Oh yes," Nancy acknowledged. "I saw those earlier. They look so… contemporary!"

Ellen rolled her eyes at the sarcasm, and turned her sights on the rest of the idols. She retrieved four more carvings and set them down next to the first one. Then she began to study them in detail.

They appeared to be primitive representations of small mammals, like monkeys without ears. These were not cute little monkeys that would be displayed on a mantel, however. These small creatures bore the menacing features of tiny warriors, their hardened eyes and wicked snarls warning of danger to their enemies. The writing that was near the bottom of each figure was unintelligible. This could have been because of the artist's shaky hand, or it could have been due to the erosion of the pieces that came with time.

Nancy joined her aside the chest, reaching for the newspaper articles that were on the floor. She unfolded them and immediately noted the date: November 12, 1913.

"Wow, Ellen," she said. "These papers should be in a local museum or something."

Ellen turned her attention away from the idols. "Why, what do they say?"

"Well, they're dated 1913." She read further down. "And it talks about a mine closing because of monster sightings."

"What?" Ellen giggled in disbelief.

"No kidding, that's what it says! It says, 'MINE CLOSED, MONSTER SIGHTINGS CLAIMED'."

"Oh, I've *got* to hear this. Read it out loud."

Nancy nodded. "All right.

"'Prospectors working the Johnson Mine near Frisco have claimed to have seen "monsters" in the mine. Despite the rumor of the Johnson Mine still producing healthy quantities of gold ore, the mine has been closed.

"'The trouble began with the disappearance of two prospectors, Marvin McKenna and John Duffy, both from Breckenridge. After a thorough search, their bodies were never recovered. Cave-ins became more frequent. And then, miners stated they had seen "small, furry monsters" living within.'"

Ellen looked over at the carved creatures, mesmerized by their wicked faces while Nancy read on.

"'Tragedy continued when these animals allegedly attacked the prospectors in the mine. When the survivors were reached, the death toll was eight.

"'As a result of this, it was decided by the mine's owner, Bartholomew Johnson, to close the mine and seal it.'"

Nancy stopped, looking up. The two women picked up the idols and contemplated.

"Do you think these are supposed to be the 'monsters' that they saw?" probed Nancy.

"Must be," Ellen replied. "Probably just folklore, though. Or maybe the old-timers' idea of a practical joke."

"What else do we have?" Nancy asked, motioning to the pile of contents.

"Just this old book," she answered. "Shall I?" Nancy nodded, and Ellen reached for the leather-bound book. Upon opening it, she found it to be a personal diary. "Wow, this will be very interesting."

Nancy leaned forward. "What is it?"

"It's a diary from some guy named Henry Johnson, dated 1913. This would be a historian's dream, reading something like this."

"Wait a minute," Nancy realized. "Edwin Johnson was the name on the snowshoes outside, right?"

Ellen nodded. "This diary must be from an old relative of the guy who lives here now."

"That's what I'm thinking."

"Some heirloom, huh?"

"Well go on, read it!" grinned Nancy, full of anticipation. "This should be intriguing."

Ellen opened the diary to a random page in the middle and began to read. "'September 30th, 1913: I have arrived at the Johnson Mine, which belongs to my father, and begun to work here. There is gold found often, though in small amounts. We work twelve hours a day, six days a week. We have nothing to keep us going save the thought of striking the mother lode and becoming rich. The winter storms should be coming soon, but we still have several weeks before the deep snow will interfere.'"

"Ooh," Nancy yawned sarcastically. "The life and times of an old miner. Not very engrossing. Skip forward and see if it says anything about little monsters."

"Okay, okay," Ellen obliged, flipping ahead until something interesting caught her eye. "Aha! Here you go. 'October 28, 1913: Most of the miners are dead. Although the blame is given to faulty bracings and clumsiness, we are doubting. Five or six of the miners survived the disaster and have all been speaking of monsters attacking them in the mine. I at first blamed hysteria, but the stories are too similar among the men. They each describe the same events, speaking of small, hairy monsters that attacked and killed some of the men. The carnage they described I must omit, in the hopes that nobody who reads this must hear the horrible recounts told to me.'" Ellen stopped and looked up at Nancy. "Is *this* engrossing enough for you?"

Nancy nodded vigorously, her eyes wide with amazement. "Oh yes, this is much better. Do you think they were *really* attacked by animals underground?"

"I don't know," shrugged Ellen. "I suppose it's possible, but I've never heard of any mountain animals like that."

Nancy suddenly became concerned. "If there *are* animals like that around here, should we get the men out of there?"

Ellen simply returned her apprehensive gaze.

9

In the tunnel below, the men had stopped at a junction. To their right was a smaller secondary tunnel, just large enough for a man to crouch through. To their left, they saw the rubble of a cave-in further down, blocking the rest of the main tunnel. John aimed his light at the pile, illuminating the rock and splintered wood that filled the spot. His light flitted across something else in the heap that caught Nick's eye.

"Hold it," Nick said. "What was that?"

John scanned the pile with his headlamp again, and found the object Nick had glimpsed. It was another stick of dynamite, like the ones they had found in the oak chest. "Whoa," John whispered. "We'd better not touch *that*."

"Damn," said Nick, stepping back. "No wonder this place caved in. These old miners weren't very cautious with their explosives, were they?"

"I guess not." John turned his light to the other tunnel. "Should we check this one out?" Nick nodded, and the men hunched down and stepped in.

They discovered that the small opening was an entrance into a huge cavern. John was the first one through, and he shined his light onto the surrounding walls. He stopped to admire the natural beauty of the cavern. Nick was right behind him, also marveling at the sight.

"Would ya look at that…" said Nick.

"This is a natural cavern," John noted. "Not part of the mine."

The cavern was fifty feet across each way, and twenty feet high. Small stalactites hung indolently from the limestone ceiling. Ground water dripped from the calcium-crusted stalactites to the floor below. As the men looked down, they could see a steep drop before them that ended abruptly with the jagged, water-carved rocks of the cavern floor.

"I don't think we need to go down there," Nick decided.

John grunted in agreement. "That probably wouldn't be a good idea." The intense cold in the cavern made him shiver. "What do you say we—"

"What was that?" Nick interrupted fearfully.

John looked down into the cavern, trying to see what had startled Nick. As the beam from his headlamp grazed the floor below, a quick burst of motion caught his attention. He gasped involuntarily and tried to follow it. A second later, his light found the source of the movement.

There was a small furry animal darting across the cavern floor. At first John thought it might be a woodchuck. But it was much leaner than a woodchuck, and definitely faster. Then it stopped, and John could see that it was something horribly different.

It had a face similar to that of a fuzzy salamander, but with large subterranean eyes and grossly oversized jaws. Its fangs rested uncomfortably on the outside of its mouth, complementing its equally large claws. John watched in amazement, and did not feel truly terrified until the beast looked directly at him and reacted.

The animal's eyes met the headlamp beam with a dull yellow reflection. It snarled at the intruders in its domain, and its gaze became a threatening glare. The animal emitted a growl and tensed its body, preparing to attack.

Suddenly the floor of the cave was alive with movement as many more of the creatures emerged from the darkness.

"Move it!" said John. "Back out of here, now!"

Nick, having also seen the mass of strange little beasts, immediately retreated. The creatures blanketed the cavern floor now, and they were screeching ferociously. They began to hastily claw their way up the incline toward the men. John scrambled behind Nick through the tight chamber opening, and back into the main tunnel.

"What the hell are we gonna do?" Nick panted, the muffled shrieks gaining volume as the creatures continued their chase. "They're coming after us!"

"I know, I know!" John scanned the main tunnel with his helmet's light, searching for the way they had come in. Then his light found the familiar rubble of the old cave-in, and he knew which way to go. "Come on, this way!"

"Wait a minute," said Nick. "What if we blow that opening closed?"

"You mean with that old dynamite?"

Nick pulled his WindBlaze cigar lighter from his coat pocket. "Why not? It's either that or try to outrun them and hope they don't claw their way through the trapdoor into the cabin!"

"Good point," agreed John. He used his headlamp to find the explosive on the ground. "Light it and run like hell!"

Nick retrieved the dynamite stick from the pile of debris, straightened the fuse, and readied his lighter. Shaking with fear, it took him several attempts to light the fuse. Finally the fuse ignited, crackling rapidly. Nick tossed the stick into the opening to the cavern, and the men ran down the tunnel as fast as they could.

An ear-shattering explosion followed, sealing the smaller tunnel. The blast also shook the main tunnel, testing its integrity. Dust and rocks fell from the timber bracings as the men ran through. The tunnel threatened to cave in, but somehow maintained its stability long enough for the men to escape.

When the men reached the mouth of the tunnel, they heard one of the bracings break behind them. Rock fell just after, thick and heavy, filling the passage.

The men scampered up the ladder and pushed the trapdoor open.

10

Ellen and Nancy jumped as the trapdoor flew open, then sighed in relief when they saw their husbands emerge from the doorway. The men stepped out of the closet and back into the living room of the cabin.

"What the hell was that explosion?" said Ellen. "We were scared to death up here!"

"You wouldn't believe us if we told you," John replied. "Let's just say nobody is going in or out of that tunnel. We had to blow it up."

"Yeah," added Nick. "There was some pretty freaky shit down there, and it needs to be kept down there."

"Little furry monsters?" Nancy said.

The men stared incredulously at her and nodded. "But how did you—"

"We've been reading this diary that was in the chest," Ellen explained. "It talks about miners being attacked by little hairy monsters. We didn't believe it, but now... what happened down there, anyway?"

The men laughed nervously. John looked at Nick, to see if he was going to tell them, who returned the same look to him.

"Um," John began, "those miners weren't kidding."

Ellen involuntarily leaned away from him. "What?"

"Yeah. We walked in quite a bit, until we were blocked by an old cave-in. We saw another stick of dynamite in the rubble."

Nancy nodded, now knowing what had caused the muffled explosion they heard and felt.

"Then we saw a smaller tunnel, off to the side, and we checked it out."

"It was an opening to a huge cavern," Nick said. "It was very cool to see. But then we saw something move on the rocks."

"I couldn't believe what I was seeing," said John. "It was like nothing I've ever seen in the animal kingdom. Lean, fast bodies, large claws, sharp teeth, and creepy yellow eyes."

"Like rats?" asked Nancy.

"Kind of," Nick said. "But they didn't have ears. You know, like lizards have earholes."

"Or salamanders," said John. "That's what their heads reminded me of. Hairy salamanders."

The women grimaced at the images they compiled in their minds.

"And all of a sudden, there were *tons* of 'em!" said Nick. "They all came after us, so we got the hell out of there. We got back to the tunnel, I lit the dynamite and put it at the opening to the cavern, and we ran for our lives."

"Then—*boom*," John said.

"That was the most frightened I've ever been in my life," said Nick. His heart was still racing.

"You poor thing," Nancy said, wrapping her arms around him.

"So," said Ellen, "are you sure the opening is sealed?"

"Oh yes," John said with conviction. "That blast shook the whole tunnel. We're lucky it didn't come down on us."

"God, John...." She held his hand lovingly, grateful that he'd made it back to her.

The group migrated to the couch to sit in front of the fire. Nick dragged the chest to where they were sitting, and began to examine its contents. He pulled out one of the rock carvings and held it up for John to see. "Look familiar?"

John recognized the figure as one of the creatures, and nodded. "Pretty flattering likeness," he remarked, "all things considered. I'll bet it wasn't easy carving this out of rock." Then his eyes went to his wife. "Hey, let me read that diary for a minute."

"Sure." Ellen handed over the old diary.

John opened it and skimmed through several random pages. He ran across some of the entries that Ellen had read earlier, regarding the attacks, and he read them out loud.

"Jesus," Nick said afterward. "Now that we've actually seen the creatures, listening to that diary is creepy."

"Absolutely." John then flipped to the last entry. "Check this out," he said. "It's from December 3rd, this year—yesterday! And in a different handwriting."

"Must be the owner of this cabin," Nancy mused. "The name on the snowshoes matches the last name on the diary. We think they're related."

John began reading the last entry aloud. "'I have traced my grandfather's footsteps to this mine on top of the mountain, which he apparently laid claim to. I have brought enough explosives to destroy the monsters that have been breeding in the mine. It took me a while to dig through to find them, but yesterday I discovered where they sleep. I will tend to them tomorrow. Once they are in hell where they belong, the soul of my grandfather, Henry Johnson, can finally rest peacefully. My work must be quick, however, as there is word of a big snowstorm coming tomorrow afternoon.'"

Ellen shifted uneasily. "He obviously did not succeed."

"The body behind the woodshed," said Nick. "Must be him."

John was in agreement. "Yeah, it must be. But how did he die? The monsters couldn't have got him, because he died outside in the snow."

The discussion was suddenly interrupted by a scuffing sound. The closet door had been left open, and the noise seemed to be coming from beneath the trapdoor. The group stared at the closet, nervously waiting to hear it again.

11

After a long spell of silence, John spoke. "Could that have been some debris falling loose down there?"

Nick shrugged. "I suppose. Should we make sure?"

"You've got to be kidding," said Nancy. "What if it's those *things* down there?"

"No way," John stated. "We blew the tunnel up so that *nothing* could get through. Hell, *we* were lucky to get through when we did!" He turned to Nick and nodded. "Let's take a look."

Nick picked up his flashlight and slowly lifted the trapdoor. John grabbed his helmet, watching with anticipation. He was ready to use it against anything that might spring from the doorway. Nothing seemed to be there, so they leaned closer and aimed their lights down the ladder.

There was still some dust from the cave-in, gently swirling in the air. Other than that, there was no motion at all.

John had to check it out. "Gimme the flashlight," he said. After receiving it from Nick, he moved into position to climb down.

"John!" Ellen whispered.

"It's okay," he assured her. "I just want to make sure everything's still stable under us."

Nick aimed the helmet's headlamp beam on the ladder while John slowly descended through the trapdoor. Once at the bottom of the ladder, John scanned the room with the flashlight. Then he aimed the light into the tunnel. He saw the fresh rock and debris from the dynamite blast. The tunnel had definitely caved in, and nothing would be coming through. John smiled in the dark and turned back toward the ladder.

He heard a noise coming from somewhere.

John stopped for a moment, wondering what he had just heard. He called to Nick. "Did you just hear something?"

A deep, vicious growl was suddenly heard, making John flinch. He drew the flashlight up to see a large animal charging out from the darkness behind the ladder. Moving on its rear legs, it was the size of a grown man. John cried out in terror.

The light revealed a hideous monster, with a face more frightening than anything out of John's worst nightmares. It was an enormous version of the small creatures they had encountered earlier, but the features were grossly magnified. It had huge, powerful jaws, almost too big for its face. More frightening, however, were its eyes. Its bulbous golden eyes burned with deadly intention, instantly striking fear into John's heart.

The monster swiped at him with its huge claws, but John spun out of the way. The creature then lost its footing on the fresh debris that littered the chamber floor. John suddenly had a brief moment to escape, and he was up the ladder instantly.

Nick slammed the trapdoor shut after John emerged, and slid the bolt to lock it. "What the hell was *that?*" he said, having seen the creature pass beneath his light.

"A-a giant version of those *things!*" stammered John. "I don't think we should stay around here," he added, fearing for their lives. "That thing is pissed off!"

A violent pounding at the trapdoor indicated that the beast was intent on breaking through.

"We have to get out of here!" Ellen cried.

"What are we going to do, run out into the blizzard?" asked Nick, his pulse also pounding.

"We can fight it off with the ski poles," offered Nancy.

"That thing would snap 'em like twigs!" said John.

Nick's eyes darted. "Has anyone seen any guns anywhere in the cabin?"

"No," they replied.

"There's more dynamite outside," stated Ellen. "That's the only real weapon we've got!"

"Works for me," said Nick, shakily digging for his cigar lighter.

A powerful limb burst through the trapdoor and sent splinters flying.

The group shrieked and sprinted for the door. They shoved the front door open, plowing through the deepening snow, and they spilled out into the fury of the snowstorm. John ran to where he had put the dynamite sticks, digging frantically to find them. He quickly uncovered two of them and brought them to Nick.

Holding the sticks together, Nick wasted no time in lighting the fuses. Then he threw the dynamite into the cabin and the group ran. The snow was up to their knees, slowing their escape into the cold.

While running, John turned around to see if their pursuer was following. Through the doorway he saw the monster shuffle into the kitchen, lumbering its way toward the opened front door.

The dynamite exploded.

The blast claimed the cabin before the monster could come out, and its force sent the four humans flying into the snow. They lay motionless in the snow for a moment, then slowly pulled themselves to their feet. They gazed in awe at what the dynamite had done to their shelter and, more importantly, to the monster. The cabin was completely destroyed. Broken boards and pieces of furry flesh were scattered on the snow around them.

John felt as though he had just been hit by a truck. "Are you all right?" he asked his wife. Ellen shrugged, then tentatively nodded. He leaned in and helped her to her feet. Turning to the others, he said, "How about you guys? You okay?"

Nick and Nancy stood up. "Yeah, I think so," said Nick. Nancy clung to his side and gave a nod. They were shaken, but they were alive.

Nick howled into the night, triumphant and relieved. The others laughed out loud to release their stress as well. They then hugged and patted each other in celebration, elated to have survived the terror. But as their adrenaline ebbed, they could feel the cold and knew there was still one more factor that needed to be addressed.

"Looks like the storm is still going strong!" John said, yelling to be heard over the rushing winds. "I think we'd better get inside the woodshed and huddle together!"

The others quickly followed him to the back of the woodshed, where Nick had broken into earlier.

They were cautious not to disturb the body behind the woodshed, although it was now completely covered by the snow. John pulled himself through the window, then helped the others as they took their turns. When they were all inside, they looked around to assess their environment.

There was only one window in the woodshed, which was fortunate. They would only have cold air coming in from that one source. Next to the piled firewood along one of the inside walls was a stack of canvas tarps.

"We can't make a fire in here," John stated. "It'd be too dangerous. The smoke probably wouldn't go outside, and we would be asphyxiated. Or we might accidentally burn this place down. Then we would have no shelter against the blizzard. We'd be dead in an hour."

"Assuming we got out of the fire," Nick added.

"You're right, a fire won't work," admitted Ellen. "We're just going to have to huddle together under those tarps to keep body heat and hope that the storm goes away by morning."

Nick couldn't help but wonder if he'd be pressing against Ellen while under the tarps.

"Can we use one of the tarps to cover the broken window?" Nancy suggested. "It would help keep the cold out."

"Excellent idea," said Nick.

The group searched the woodshed for a means of attaching the tarp to the window.

Their search was interrupted by the sound of scratching.

"What the hell is that?" John asked fearfully.

They looked around and quickly realized that the sound was coming from beneath the plywood in the middle of the woodshed floor.

"Oh my God," Nick blurted, suddenly understanding. "The guy outside died on his way from here *to* the cabin! They must've wounded him, he got away, and lived just long enough to cover the hole and lock this shed up from the outside." He took several steps back from the plywood. "That board is covering a mineshaft, remember? We thought we sealed the monsters off, but we forgot about this opening here. Now this is the only place they can go in and out!"

As the grim realization set in among the group, the frenzy of clawing intensified under the plywood.

12

The board was ripped to pieces and nudged aside. A swarm of furry, grimy animals spilled out from the mouth of the mineshaft. Their long teeth, claws, and soulless eyes were a horrifying sight.

"*Jesus!*" screamed Nancy.

"Oh fuck no!" John exclaimed. He kicked at them, trying to knock them back into the hole. After booting a couple away, another one of them clung to John's boot with its claws. John shook his leg feverishly, but the animal was dug in. Then it began its scamper up John's leg, puncturing him with its claws. John cried out and backhanded the animal, feeling its cold, bristly fur. The force dislodged it and sent it aside.

Nick and the women shrank back as the animals scuttled toward them. There was nowhere to retreat to inside the woodshed.

"Out the window!" said Nick. He then pulled himself up and quickly squirmed through the opening.

John moved to join the others, continuing to kick at the beasts to keep them at bay. But there were just so many.

"Go!" John blurted, grabbing Ellen. He lifted her high enough for her to work her way out the window. He pushed to get her through. He would send Nancy through next.

The monsters overtook her. Nancy shrieked hysterically as the horde of little beasts dug into her legs and tugged her across the ground.

Turning his eyes to see, John yelled, "No!" He lunged toward her, but it was too late.

The swarm crawled down the mineshaft with Nancy in their grip. Her terror-stricken face and flailing hands disappeared into the opening.

"*Nancy!*" cried Nick, watching from outside the window.

Her screams echoed in the darkness below.

A dozen of the animals remained back, hoping for more than one victim. They advanced at John.

He reached over to the pile next to him and grabbed a couple of logs. Then he hurled them at the little monsters, buying precious seconds.

"Come on!" pleaded Ellen from the other side. Her hands beckoned for John.

John wasted no time launching himself at the window. His legs kicked as he climbed through, trying to find something to push off of.

Ellen and Nick took hold of his arms and yanked him outside. They hurried to their feet and away from the woodshed, keeping their eyes on the window.

They stood in the open for five minutes. The wind and snow pelted them while they watched to see if the creatures were going to come out for them.

It seemed they would not.

Ellen finally spoke. "What now?"

"We have to go after Nancy," said John.

"You—you want to go after her?" Nick said. "Down into their mine?"

"No, I don't *want* to," admitted John. "But we can't… leave her."

"Fuck that! I'm not going back in there!" The terror in Nick's voice was powerful.

"She's your *wife!*" Ellen charged.

Nick loved his wife, but fear got the better of him. He didn't even feel like a man at the moment. But that was better than another encounter with those creatures. "I'm not going back in there!" he repeated.

"What else can we do?" posed Ellen.

"I say we try to make it down the mountain," Nick said fervently.

John shook his head. "There's no way we'd make it before we froze to death. It took us three hours to get up here!"

"But that was *skiing!* We could *run* down the mountain."

"You're not thinking clearly. There's just too much snow! You could stumble, break a leg, get stuck in a drift of deep snow… or just lose all your energy and drop before you're halfway down. Hell, we're losing body temperature by the minute right now!"

"I don't want to go back in *there!*" said Nick, pointing to the woodshed.

"One thing's for sure," said Ellen. "We'll freeze to death out *here*. And it's gonna be dark soon."

The group looked at each other, seeing equal dread in their eyes.

Nick was panicked. "Well—what if those things were to come back? We don't even have any weapons!"

"Let's get the rest of the dynamite," suggested John.

"Are you crazy? How the hell would *those* help us at all?"

"Well, at least we'd take a bunch of 'em with us. Or, hopefully, we'll use them to seal the tunnels behind us after we find Nancy."

Nick realized John was right. But they would need more weaponry to fight the creatures. He looked over at the demolished cabin. "Maybe we can find something to use that survived the explosion."

"Yes, good idea," said Ellen. "Even if it's just a flashlight. Or our ski poles."

"And anything we can use to climb; any kind of rope," John prompted.

"There was some in the woodshed," Ellen announced. "I saw it hanging on the wall."

Shivering, Nick started toward the cabin's wreckage. John and Ellen were right behind him. The trio approached the site, and then began rooting around the debris for anything useful.

"Found the flashlight," Ellen reported. The men grunted approvingly. A few seconds later, Ellen spotted one of the straps of Nick's backpack. She grabbed it and wrested the backpack free from under a log section. "And a backpack!"

"Great!" said Nick, coming over to inspect the contents. He dug inside and pulled out his hand axe. He was grateful to see that thing; he held onto it tightly.

"Check this out!" said John. "It's the pickaxe from the mining chest! Or at least what's left of it." He held it up for the others to see. The handle had been blown off by the dynamite blast, leaving a shredded stump of wood lodged in the eye of the pickaxe head.

"It can still be a weapon," Ellen acknowledged.

John held it like a dagger. "Yep."

"Here's a ski pole," said Nick. "Oh, and a couple more!"

"Grab 'em," John said.

After a thorough search of the area, they were disappointed to find nothing else that could be of any use to them. John made sure to remember the dynamite in the snow, and he went to the spot to dig it out. He burrowed through the new snowfall and pulled out the four remaining sticks of dynamite. Then he turned to Nick.

"You still have your lighter?"

Nick patted his pocket, feeling the cigar lighter inside. "Yeah."

"All right then."

John and the others headed back to the woodshed. It was an unsettling feeling; the anticipation of being shielded from the elements combined with the fear of being attacked again by the dangerous animals. But now they had something to fight them off with.

They circled around the shed and to the lone window in the back. Looking at each other, the group prepared themselves for going inside.

"Trade me?" said John, offering the pickaxe head to Nick. "I'd do better with yours."

Nick was happy to trade his hand axe for the longer piece. "Sure," he said, and the men swapped weapons.

"All right," John said quietly, "here we go."

He popped his head through the window. Scanning the shed, he saw nothing moving. The animals had retreated to where they came from. He crawled inside, keeping the axe in one hand, and got to his feet.

"Okay," he whispered. "Coast is clear."

Thank God, thought Ellen. She couldn't stand being in that freezing wind any longer. She pushed herself through the opening and into the shelter of the woodshed.

Nick passed the ski poles through the window. When they were taken from him, he hauled himself up and through the opening.

Everybody was relieved that the monsters were gone. They grabbed one of the tarps, careful to not make much noise, and huddled together beneath it. After a while, their teeth had stopped chattering and feeling had begun to return to their fingers and toes.

Inevitably, they had to begin their search for Nancy.

"Come on," said John. "We have to figure out how we're gonna get down there to her."

Ever so quietly, the trio approached the mouth of the mineshaft.

13

The group peered down into the hole. They could not see the bottom.

"How far down do you think it is?" Ellen wondered.

Nick's flashlight beam cut into the darkness, but wherever the bottom was, it was dark enough that the light didn't reflect off of anything visible. "Can't tell," said Nick.

"Only one way to find out," said John.

His eyes found the roll of rope hanging on one of the walls. He pulled it down and unraveled it. To their disappointment, there was only about ten feet of rope.

"Well, that's not gonna do us any good," he sighed.

Ellen's eyes closed. "Shit."

There definitely wasn't enough rope to use for a descent. John suddenly had an idea, though.

"We need to cut the rope into sections," he announced. "Then we can tie the tarps together, diagonally, and climb down on them."

Looking at the large grommet holes in the tarps' corners, Nick realized that plan could work. "How do we cut the rope?" he inquired.

"Your axe," said John. He handed the tool back to its owner.

"Of course," said Nick. "Duh." He took the hand axe and held it ready. "Where do we cut?"

"Let's see," John said, calculating. "We've got four tarps. So we'll need three pieces in between, and then one at the top to tie off to something. I guess just cut it into fourths."

"Okay." Nick laid the rope out straight on the hard ground. He estimated the length and started chopping. It took several swings, but his axe was sharp enough to cleave the rope. He pulled it along and made the other cuts.

John dragged the tarps over and helped Nick tie them together with the sections of rope. Within minutes, they connected the tarps together, corner to corner. The chain of tarps had a total length of over thirty feet.

"That's much better," John said. "Now we have something like thirty feet." There was a dose of pride in his voice. He'd come up with a brilliant idea to use what was available to them.

"Will that be long enough?" Ellen wondered.

"We'll see," said John, shrugging. "We'll secure the tarp-line to something, and one of us will climb down and see how far down it is."

"I don't like it," said Ellen.

"I don't see any other way," said John.

Even Nick knew that would have to be their course of action. "It's our best chance to get down there."

"Where can we tie it to?" John mumbled, looking around.

"How about that big hook it was hanging from?" said Nick.

John studied the hook that was screwed into the wooden wall. It was about half an inch thick and did indeed look like it could support the weight of a person and the tarps. "Sure," he said. "Tie it up there."

Nick secured the end segment of rope around the hook and made the knot tight. "Okay," he said.

John slid the tail of the chain into the mineshaft. Kicking the canvas with his foot, he caused it to lengthen down the rocky walls and hang there. He waited for a minute, wondering if some of the creatures would latch onto the tarp chain and come up to attack. When nothing happened, John readied himself for the climb.

"One at a time," John insisted. "We want to keep the weight to a minimum for the tarps and rope."

"Agreed," said Nick.

"All right, let's do this," said John. "I'll go first."

"I'll go right after you," Nick stated.

"And I'll go after Nick," said Ellen.

John was quick to respond. "No. You stay up here."

"Forget it, John," she said defiantly. "There's no way I'm letting you go down there without me."

"Look—"

"Forget it," she repeated, hand on hips. "Nancy's my friend too."

John knew he wasn't going to win this argument. "Okay," he conceded.

"Here," said Nick, handing his axe to John. "We need to arm ourselves with everything before we go down."

"Damn right," John said. "Chances are, we're gonna have to deal with those little monsters somewhere in there."

"Even worse, there may be more of the big ones," said Nick. "Like that huge—den-father—or whatever it was."

John's skin tightened. "God, I hope not. We'd need a shotgun for that."

Ellen kissed her husband. "Ready?"

John nodded. "Yep." Then, after a sigh, he tucked the hand axe in his beltline and took hold of the musty tarp.

Nick handed the flashlight to him. "Don't drop this," he warned. "That's our only source of light. And it's getting dark outside."

"I won't drop it," John promised. He would hold onto it like a priceless gem. He gripped the canvas with his free hand and stepped over the perimeter's railroad ties. Then, looking down, he began working his way down the tarps.

Wrapping around the material, John lowered himself as if he was sliding down a fire station pole. He did so slowly, patiently; he did not want to lose control of his pace.

He looked up at the square of light above. His partners were watching anxiously. John resumed his descent, aiming the flashlight downward. Then, to his relief, the light beam showed him a rocky floor.

"I see the bottom!" he called as quietly as possible.

Nick smiled. "The tarps were long enough after all?"

"Yes, just barely. That was lucky." John set foot on the ground and panned the light around.

There was a mass of knotted rope on the floor. Beyond that was a tunnel leading away, somewhat in the old cabin's direction. And it was cold down there. The excavated rock felt like ice. Thankfully, no animals were in sight.

"Okay," said John. "You're next."

Nick gently placed the sticks of dynamite in his coat pockets. Then, using both hands, he went down the length of tarps to join John at the bottom. It took him only two minutes to travel the thirty-five feet to the tunnel floor.

"All right," said John. He moved Nick back and called up to his wife. "Drop the ski poles, honey. And the pickaxe head."

"Okay," Ellen said. "Stand back."

The men stepped back into the tunnel. "We're clear."

She gathered the poles and dropped them straight down, one by one. Hearing them clack on the rocky floor below, she got a sense of how far down the men were. When she dropped the pickaxe head, she cringed when she heard the loud clang of the heavy iron landing on rock.

Everything they had was down there now. Ellen had free use of her hands to climb down the tarp chain. The first step over the railroad ties was shaky. Gripping the tarp, she began to descend into the mineshaft.

"Doing good, honey," John said from the bottom. "Slow and easy."

She continued down, her eyes skipping over the random shades and shapes of the carved rock. She had to take occasional glances down the tarp, though, to see how much farther she had to go.

When she was about three feet away from the ground, something happened to the tarp line. Suddenly it was no longer taut; it released down the shaft.

Ellen dropped the final three feet, but didn't land hard. She toppled over upon landing, and the string of tarps came down on top of her.

John rushed to her. "Ellen! Are you okay?"

She stood up and brushed herself free. "Yeah, I'm okay. That was close, huh?"

The men nodded. "Yeah," said John. He was thankful that his wife was all right, but at the same time, his heart was racing with panic. With the tarps fallen, the group was stuck at the bottom of the shaft.

14

"You said the knot was secure!" John hissed to Nick.

"It was," Nick whispered back, "I swear! Maybe the rope was old, dry, whatever, and just broke."

"Regardless," said Ellen, trying to prevent an argument, "at least it got us all down here." She looked up the shaft to the top, which looked extremely far away. "Getting back up, however... I don't think is gonna happen."

Nick's pulse quickened. "We have to get back up there."

"Not gonna happen," John muttered.

"What if—what if we tie the tarps to a pole and throw it back up?"

"What, like a spear?" said Ellen, her voice thick with skepticism.

"Yeah. Maybe it could land on the corner and catch."

Ellen looked at the pile of heavy tarps. "There's no way you could throw a pole up that would carry that weight."

"And even if you could," added John, "no ski pole would hold up against the weight of a person climbing up. It would snap."

"What's that?" Ellen asked, pointing to the pile of knotted rope.

"I dunno," said John. "Must've been put here by the cabin's owner."

"Maybe cut and thrown in after he climbed up to escape the animals."

John nodded. "That would make sense, not wanting them to be able to climb up the rope after him. And then, for good measure, he covered up the mineshaft and locked the woodshed door."

Fearing they were trapped there forever, Nick fought to control his rushing heartbeat. The last thing he needed was to have a panic attack. "Well, there *has* to be another way out," he reasoned. "I'm sure of it. The miners had to have more places to get their stuff in and out. You know, in case of cave-ins and such?"

"We'll find out," said John. "We have to move anyway, in order to find Nancy."

"So how do we do this?" Ellen asked, her eyes nervously watching for movement in the tunnel.

"I dunno," John replied. "Should we call out to her?"

"Those things would hear us," said Nick. His voice was tight.

"I know, I know." John pondered their next move. "Let's just figure it out as we go. Get your weapons ready, hold onto 'em tight, and follow me."

They picked up everything from the ground around them and held what they had as their weapons.

John offered Nick his flashlight back. "You want to lead the way?" asked John.

Nick declined, waving his hands in front of him. "Go right ahead."

"Okay." John turned the light on the tunnel ahead. Clenching the hand axe, he began down the cold tunnel.

Nick and Ellen stayed right on his tail. Each of them wielded a ski pole, and Nick had the pickaxe head ready in his other hand.

"Look," said John, illuminating the floor.

The others looked where he was shining the light. Dark spatters of shiny liquid speckled the ground.

"Is that… blood?" said Ellen.

"Yes, I think so," Nick replied. "Oh God…."

"There's not very much," John pointed out, trying to stay positive. "Just enough to know she was getting scratched up by their claws as they took her. Not enough blood loss to be life-threatening."

"No?" Nick said feebly.

"No."

"Okay. I hope you're right."

"Come on," John prompted. "Let's find her."

John kept the flashlight aimed at the floor before them. The light revealed occasional beds of nickel and copper within the rock. They were deep inside the subterranean rock. It was deathly quiet in the tunnel, the air being muffled by the dense rock covering them.

Then they heard something.

The crew stopped in their tracks, everyone listening.

What was that? Nick wanted to say. But he didn't dare open his mouth.

Again the noise, echoing from somewhere further in. It sounded like a chirping, a barking. The group couldn't quite tell where it was coming from. They stayed quiet, not wanting to let the creatures know where they were in the tunnel.

The noises ceased, and it was quiet once more.

"Come on," John whispered after a long silence. "Let's keep going."

They pushed forward. Whether they were going to encounter the little monsters or not, they had to try their best to find Nancy. Especially if she was still alive.

Nick was hoping to hear his wife. He listened for any sort of scream, cry, or whimper that could aid them in locating her. But so far, not a peep. Nick prayed that she was just unconscious.

The feeling of claustrophobia crept over Ellen. The air seemed heavy. She felt trapped, helpless. "John?" she said. "I'm starting to freak out."

Her husband understood. "I know, love. Me too. But we'll be okay. There has to be more than one way out, like Nick said."

"It's like it's hard to breathe. And my heart's beating faster."

The words instilled panic in Nick. His mind allowed the dread to take him also. "Shit," was all he could say.

John stopped and looked at them. "Don't have a panic attack. Take a long, deep breath," he calmly instructed. "Both of you. You just need to center yourself. Relax. Breathe. We're okay."

Ellen and Nick did as he suggested. A minute later, they had regained control of their senses.

"We'll be okay," John repeated. "There's plenty of air. And that tells me that there are more ways to get to the surface."

Ellen nodded. "All right. Let's keep moving."

John met eyes with Nick. "Ready?"

"Yeah," said Nick.

"Let's go get your wife."

15

As they moved deeper into the mine, they watched the ground where they stepped. They didn't want to catch any rock crumbles wrong and roll an ankle. The flashlight beam scanned the rough rock walls and cracked support beams bracing the tunnel every ten feet.

"If we only had a map," said Nick. "I have no idea where we are right now."

"That's why we're gonna keep moving," John responded. "We're not gonna stop until we find Nancy and then find a way out."

"There *must* be other ways out," Ellen added, although her tone was not as confident as her statement.

They pressed on, keeping their voices at a whisper.

"Do you think they took her back to that cavern we first saw them in?" wondered John.

Nick shook his head. "Naw, we blasted that shut."

"But they found a way to get to the woodshed," John pointed out. "So there has to be another way to their lair."

"Or maybe there's more than one lair," said Nick.

John doubted it. "I would think a large number of creatures like that would all live together in one pack. Mating, hunting, feeding—" He quickly decided to stop talking along those lines, assuming Nancy was their intended meal.

Nick already knew. There was no other reason for the creatures to take her. He had little hope of finding her alive, especially considering they hadn't heard any screams or yells echoing throughout the tunnels. But the group had to search for her, just in case she was somehow alive.

They continued further into the earth. The air within the mine tasted stale, musty. It left the tang of cold rock in their saliva. If the group weren't so focused on bracing for vicious animals, they would realize how thirsty they were.

They arrived at a fork that split into two tunnels. John turned to the others. "Which way should we go?" he asked.

"Let's try the one on the right," said Nick. "I guess."

"'Kay." John headed down the tunnel on the right. He led the trio through the rock, staying quiet in order to hear any animals coming for them. They moved about forty feet, and then John noticed something.

"Do you feel that?"

"Yeah," said Nick. "Feels like a breeze."

"Come on." John continued forward.

After twenty more feet, they saw the slightest bit of light. It was a faint beacon, but it was definitely light hitting the rock of the tunnel.

"Daylight!" John said excitedly.

Ellen wanted to cry from the wave of relief that washed over her; they had found a way out of the mine. Eagerly, they followed the light to an opening in the rock.

"Thank God," Nick sighed. "Thank God."

The group gazed out at the tumultuous blizzard, which continued to bury the mountaintop with snow. About fifty feet away, they could still see some of the cabin wreckage. Daylight was fading, however, as the sun was setting for the night.

"All right," said John. "At least we found a way out."

It was a huge relief knowing they had an escape route. The fear and panic of claustrophobia was lifted now, and the group was grateful. They weren't happy about being inside a mine with hundreds of dangerous animals, but at least now they knew they weren't trapped there. They had found a way out.

"Okay," said Nick. "I guess we go back to the fork and go left instead."

"Right," John nodded. He looked over at his wife. "You can stay here where it's safe, love."

Ellen shook her head. "No way, baby. If you're going in there, I'm going to be at your side."

John was surprised that she didn't choose to remain at the opening. "You sure?"

"Yeah. I mean, what if I stayed here and those things found me alone?"

"Then you run away into the snow."

"They might chase me down. I might get stuck in the snow. I think we all have a better chance against them by staying together."

He couldn't argue that logic. "All right," he conceded, giving her a kiss. "Let's keep looking for Nancy together."

They turned around and took the tunnel back into the hillside.

"Just make sure we find *this* tunnel again," Ellen commented. Her tone reflected the seriousness of her statement.

"We should mark our trail," said Nick, "to make sure we don't get lost again trying to get out."

Ellen nodded. "That's a good idea. But how?"

John looked around, his eyes settling on the wooden bracing timbers framing the tunnels. He raised a ski pole and tried to carve an X into the old wood. The result was unsuccessful; the wood was too hard.

"Use the axe," Nick suggested. "Coupl'a whacks oughta make a visible X."

"Hell yeah." John took aim with the hand axe, chopped to cut a good groove in the wood's bottom corner, then tilted the axe the other way and finished the mark.

"Good," said Ellen. "We'll be able to follow our X's out of here."

They returned to the fork. This time, obviously, they would choose the tunnel on the left.

John continued to mark the timbers with X's as they passed. Flashlight firm in hand, he led the others through the cold darkness. The light beam showed the way.

Something caught John's eye in the moving beam. Taking a better look, he noticed more spatters of blood on the rocky floor.

"Looks like more blood," said Nick. His voice was weak; he knew where the blood had come from.

"You're right," John whispered. "We must be going the right way."

The group exchanged glances, each finding dread in the faces of the others.

"Keep your weapons tight," said John once more. Then he continued walking.

Silently, they moved forward, following the crimson trail.

16

They snuck through the tunnel, noting that it wound to the left. The curve was subtle, so at least they could still see ahead of them enough to prepare for a surprise around a corner. After fifty more feet, they saw something square-shaped on the ground.

"Is that... an old can?" Ellen whispered.

"Looks like it," said John. There was a rectangular five-gallon container, made of rusting metal, with a round screw-off cap.

"Probably kerosene," Nick figured. "Used for lanterns back in the mining days."

When they got to the can, John picked it up and gave it a little shake. The group heard a liquid sloshing around inside. "Feels about half full," said John.

"See what it is," Ellen prompted.

Her husband tried to unscrew the cap, but it was stuck. "Damn." He tapped on it a few times with the blunt end of the hand axe. Maybe he could knock loose any rust or corrosion that was binding it shut. He tried again with his hand. No luck.

Ellen commented unnecessarily. "Stuck, huh?"

John was not going to give up. He had strong hands and a good grip; he should be able to open this tin container. Breathing in, he clutched the cap while holding the can firmly. He strained until the cap reluctantly began to move. John unscrewed it, smirking triumphantly. He leaned in to take a whiff and quickly pulled back his face.

"Yep, that's kerosene, all right."

"We should bring that with us," said Nick.

John nodded. "Yeah. Maybe we can make torches to protect us."

"Against those things?" Ellen doubted.

"They're underground creatures," said John. "The fire would hurt their sensitive eyes. And besides, I think *all* animals are afraid of fire."

"Good point."

"Find us some wood we can use for torches," said Nick.

John moved the flashlight along the bracings and the area around. Some fragments of wood lay on the ground, but nothing substantial. "Shit," he mumbled.

Nick offered any suggestion he could. "Maybe you can hack something free from the edges? Like, maybe a couple feet long?"

"What about these?" Ellen said, holding up a ski pole.

As soon as the flashlight beam hit the pole, John saw the same idea she had. "Of course! That'll work. We just need some cloth to wrap around the end and be lit." John removed his stocking cap.

"Don't burn *that*," said Ellen. "You'll need it to cover your head if we go back into the snowstorm."

"What, then?"

"Um, are you wearing a T-shirt under those layers?"

John nodded. "Yeah. Here, hold this," he said, handing her the flashlight. Then, he set the fuel can on the floor and unzipped his parka. He shed the coat, pulled his flannel shirt off, and then removed his T-shirt. Now he could really tell how icy cold it was inside the mine. He hurriedly put the rest of his clothing back on.

"Shit, it's cold!" he spat. He rubbed his arms to try to make them warmer.

"Here," said Nick, holding out his hand. "Gimme that, and I'll rip it into strips."

John passed the shirt to him and watched as Nick started ripping it at an armpit seam. Within seconds, Nick had ripped the shirt into several long, ragged sections. Then he took one, wrapped it around the basket end of his ski pole, and tied it together.

"There," he said. "Now, just a little dousing in the kerosene."

"Let me do mine," said Ellen. She reached for and received a strip of the cotton shirt.

John took one as well, and he began to wrap it around the end of his pole. Then he picked up the container of kerosene and prepared to pour.

"Now remember," he warned. "This stuff is highly flammable, so be careful. We don't want the torches to put out too much smoke, especially inside a small tunnel."

"And kerosene smoke is very thick," Nick added.

"So, just a little?" said Ellen.

"Just a little." John tilted the can, letting the petroleum liquid dribble out through the opening. He wasn't sure just how much kerosene would be needed to keep their makeshift torches burning, but he was going to play it safe. He wanted to start with a smaller amount and see how that did. He splashed enough kerosene to just wet the whole wrap.

"Try that," said John. "See if that's enough."

Nick pulled his lighter from his pocket. Holding the pole away from them, he struck the lighter and brought it to the cloth. It ignited completely. The flame looked like it was going to keep burning a while.

"I think that's good," said Nick.

"All right." John doused his and Ellen's cloth wraps. Then the couple touched theirs with Nick's, lighting them from his fire. The tunnel brightened up considerably.

"That's much better," Nick remarked.

"Now you can turn off the flashlight," said Ellen, "to save the batteries."

John shook his head. "I'm keeping the flashlight on. Its light shoots farther than that of the torches. And we'll want to see as far ahead of us as we can."

"I second that," Nick stated, reaching out to relieve John of the fuel canister.

They pushed on, hacking the forward sides of the bracing beams with X's to make sure their return route was marked. The light from the torches aided their vision. And the little bit of heat coming from the fire felt good on their faces.

John stopped. "There's some more."

The others looked in the direction of the flashlight beam and saw more crimson stains on the ground. It was more than just drips; it was a big splash. Each person knew that the likelihood of Nancy still being alive was slim.

Nick's fear was turning into anger. "If we find their lair," he said, "we can use the rest of the kerosene to burn them all."

Ellen was a fan of that plan. "Works for me."

John held up the can and shook it. "I don't think there's enough left for something like that. I don't know, it depends on how big their lair is."

"True. If it's the size of that cavern we found earlier," Nick pointed out, "there'd be no way we could get it all burning."

"Come on, let's keep moving."

They kept a slow, steady pace, staying as quiet as they could. There was noise coming from ahead, something like the chattering of many animals. It made the group fearful, knowing what terrible things were making those sounds.

Ellen strained her ears, hoping to hear any sound from Nancy over the chatter. She was saddened that she didn't. With any luck at all, Nancy was just unconscious.

The path led to an opening in the rock, similar to the one the men had discovered earlier that day.

John stepped into it first, holding the torch pole and flashlight in one hand and the hand axe tightly in the other.

17

There was a cavern on the other side. Large and hollow, and the noise from the colony of beasts echoed throughout.

John shined the flashlight around to scan the cavern. He saw the familiar view of the cavern they'd seen, as well as another opening across from them on the top of the slope.

This is the same cavern we saw earlier, John noted. *Except we were on the opposite side up there*.

He walked further inside. The others followed closely, holding their makeshift torches at their perimeter.

The light was noticed by the animals, and they started screeching with energy.

"Watch it," said John. "Be ready if they come."

Within seconds, the floor was alive with the little creatures. They appeared in the light from the group's torches and flashlight. They advanced slowly, apprehensive of the fire. But their intent was certain; they were determined to get to the intruders and kill them. The light reflected in their eyes as yellow glares of hate.

"Stay away!" screeched Ellen. She desperately waved her torch at them.

The men jabbed and swung their torches as well, warding the beasts off. John aimed the flashlight into as many subterranean eyes as he could. The results were successful, and the animals reluctantly kept their distance.

"Pour the gas," said John. "We'll light it to keep them away with a fire barrier."

Nick wasted no time emptying the remaining kerosene from the can onto the rocky floor between them and the beasts.

"Light it!" Ellen belted.

The group took a step back. Nick stretched his arm to light the lighter, and the flame made contact with the vapors rising from the liquid.

The cavern was illuminated instantly. Screeches of protest echoed throughout; surely the light was painful for the animals' sensitive eyes. They scurried away to a safer distance.

The light exposed Nancy, or what was left of her. She was half eaten, her dead eyes still open.

Nick's legs wobbled. "We're too late," he sobbed.

She had been devoured. Her leg tissue and most of her torso was gone, leaving much of her sticky red skeleton showing.

"Oh, God," sobbed Nick. "Ohh…."

Stricken with grief, he wanted to drop to the ground.

"I'm so sorry, Nick," Ellen whimpered. She was shaking.

"Me too, man," said John.

Moments later, the kerosene on the ground burned up, leaving smoking rock.

Then Nick's torch went out. The cloth he had used was all burned up. He stiffened; this was a cause for alarm.

John and Ellen realized that their torches would also expire at any minute.

Ellen's heart was thumping rapidly. "W-What do we do?"

"I don't know," John whispered. "Maybe if we just back out of here they'll go back to their meal and leave us alone." After the words came out, he hated that he referred to Nancy as *meal*. It was harsh, but true. And hopefully that's what would happen.

Ellen gripped Nick's arm. "Come on."

Nick nodded and wiped his dribbling nose.

They backed their way out of the cavern. Calmly. Smoothly. No sudden movements to trigger a chase. In just a few seconds, they would be out of the cavern and in the tunnel.

Ellen's fire died.

"Almost there," John murmured. Then his torch was out as well. "Shit…."

The flashlight beam continued weaving on the rocky floor. The group could hear the chatter of the beasts become more animated, but they were not yet coming for their prey.

"*Gogogo!*" Nick hissed. They backed through the opening and into the mine tunnel.

Stepping away, Ellen's eyes were fixed on the opening. She watched earnestly, anxiously. She was afraid to even blink.

Please, God, prayed John, *just stay in there, go back to your meal, and keep eating.*

The creatures did not do as John hoped. They appeared in the flashlight beam, charged the opening, and came for the humans.

"Run!" he screamed.

John flipped the light beam 180 degrees and broke into a run with his comrades. Their flight drew more aggressive screeches from the pursuers.

Panting, Nick reached into his coat for the dynamite. He pulled out all four sticks and prepared to light them.

John suddenly heard more screeches coming from straight ahead. He stopped; apparently there were deadly animals coming at them from both ends of the tunnel. He turned, and the flashlight caught Nick working his lighter.

"Wait!" John cried. "Don't light it, they've got us cornered!"

"What?" shrieked Ellen.

Nick was panicked. "What do we do, then? Fight 'em all?"

The light found a shallow pocket in the rock that had only been carved out a few feet. "In there," said John.

They crammed themselves into the pocket, out of the tunnel's straightway, and shrank themselves back as much as possible.

The sounds were louder, closer. From both sides.

"Oh my God," Ellen burbled.

"There's way too many of them," said Nick. "We can't fight them all."

The trio cowered in the dark pocket while the creatures were closing in from both sides.

18

Nick knew what he had to do.

It was his idea to ski to the top of the mountain today. It was partially his fault for not checking the weather forecast. Because of him, they were all stuck on the mountain, facing their deaths in the mine. And, because of him, Nancy was already dead.

His wife, his partner, his friend. Without her, he could never be the same again.

"I'm gonna lead them all back to the cavern," he stated. "When they chase after me, wait until they all pass by, and then hurry on to the surface!"

"What?" said Ellen. "They'll kill you!"

"Not until I take them with me." Nick held up the sticks of dynamite.

John looked at him, seeing the vengeful duty in his eyes. He wasn't quite Nick anymore.

Ellen didn't say a word. She had no idea how to respond to Nick's plan. It was the only way any of them might get out alive, but it was heartrending to know that Nick was on his way to die.

"Okay? Go once they've all followed me inside!"

"Good luck, man," said John, not knowing what else to say.

Nick took the flashlight, stepped out from the pocket in the rock, and swung the light beam around.

A horde of mangy little beasts was coming fast from the outbound end of the tunnel.

"Jesus!" Nick ran for the mouth of the cavern. The flashlight beam found a swarm of creatures spilling out from the opening.

No! You're not stopping me until I get you all together in the cavern!

With a war cry, he waded into the oncoming animals, immediately feeling their piercing claws on his legs. Nick ran on resolutely, carrying a mass of them into the cavern.

***

The second group of beasts raced by the pocket in pursuit.

John and Ellen clutched each other tightly, praying they would not be discovered by the passing creatures.

The animals zipped by on their way to the den.

My God, Nick's idea worked, thought John.

Ellen dug into her coat to get her phone, knowing they would need the flashlight app.

John waited a few seconds, until it sounded like the tunnel was vacant. "Go!" he whispered urgently.

Ellen turned on the phone, thanked her maker that it still had power, and activated the flashlight app. John held onto her parka while the two of them ran the escape route. Their breathing was rushed and loud in their heads. Ellen made sure to spot each X on the timbers as they ran under them.

***

A frenzy of claws shredded Nick. He fought the beasts off as best he could; he had to endure them until they were all inside the lair. When he saw the rest of the creatures flood into the cavern, he knew it was time to destroy the entire colony.

Nick quickly dropped the flashlight to free that hand. He pulled the dynamite with one hand and grabbed his lighter with the other. Fighting through the pain from the clawing and biting, Nick focused on lighting the fuses. They sputtered to life from the flame of his cigar lighter. For a split second, he found it funny that the trusty WindBlaze torch lighter he purchased for forty dollars was now absolutely priceless.

Holding two sticks of fizzling dynamite in each hand, Nick cried out to the darkness.

The creatures were all over him, but he refused to let go of the explosives. His cries evolved into screams of pain and fury.

Suddenly, a face appeared in the faint light from the burning fuses. Nick's heart froze.

It was another large monster, likely the mate of the one they blew up in the cabin. This one was slightly larger, probably the male. It opened its wide maw, exposing terrible teeth, and roared with rage. It was the face of a devil.

Nick laughed defiantly, madly.

The dynamite exploded, taking all life and collapsing the cavern.

***

Ellen yelped hearing the explosion. She could feel the entire mine shake. Dust rained down from the bracings.

"Ohmygodohmygod!" she stammered. "I don't wanna die in here!"

"Move!" said John, pushing her faster.

They scurried through the tunnel, back to the fork, and into the right tunnel. There was still rumbling behind them from falling rock loosened by the blast.

When the couple made it to the surface, they stopped to catch their breath and calm their hearts.

"We made it," John panted. "We made it."

"Yeah... thank God."

He looked around. "It sure is getting dark quickly."

Ellen nodded. "We better return to the woodshed for shelter."

They emerged from the mouth and started trudging through the snow. Heading for the woodshed, they winced from the wind blasting their faces. It was imperative to get to shelter from the storm until morning.

They made it to the woodshed and rounded it to the lone window. Then John boosted Ellen up and through the opening before climbing in after her.

Ellen glanced around the woodshed's interior. There was nothing left to help them stay warm; the tarps were gone, at the bottom of the mineshaft.

"How do we keep from freezing to death?" she asked. "Nothing in here except firewood. Are we gonna cover ourselves under a blanket of logs?" A chuckle accompanied her question.

John raised an eyebrow. *That might not be a bad idea,* he thought. *Anything to insulate our bodies would be helpful.* He smiled. "Actually, yeah. That's exactly what we'll do. It couldn't hurt, after all."

Ellen shrugged, willing to do anything that might save them. "Okay."

"First, though," said John, "we'll need to huddle together under our coats. We can put them together like one cocoon. Then we'll add a layer of wood."

"All right. Let's get some wood together."

John set the flashlight on the ground, aiming it to where they could see the mineshaft and avoid falling in. They approached the stack of chopped wood and pulled some of the larger and lighter pieces down.

Then they unzipped their parkas and combined them into one larger cover to share body heat. It even partially covered their heads. Their hands snuck out from underneath and placed the split wood pieces on top of them. Once they had done everything they could, they huddled together and clung to each other to retain body heat.

"So cold," Ellen murmured. "Hard to breathe."

"Just keep holding me, baby," said John, keeping them together tightly. "It'll be a long night, but we'll make it through to morning."

We've got to.

***

When John snapped awake, he noticed the sunlight beaming in through the window. *Thank God*, he thought.

"Ellen, wake up," he said. "Wake up, baby."

Her eyelids fluttered open wearily. "What?"

"It's morning. We made it."

Ellen acknowledged the light and she sighed. "Oh thank God. Is it still snowing?"

John leaned forward and listened. "I don't hear any wind."

Slowly getting to her feet, Ellen said, "Let's have a look." She shuffled to the window and peered out.

The valley was covered in thick snow, glistening white under the rays of the rising sun. The clouds were dissipating and the sky was turning blue.

"Oh thank God," she sighed. "The storm is over."

"Really?" John got up, instantly noticing how stiff his body was. He approached the window frame and gazed out. "Wow," he muttered. "Look at all that snow."

"How deep do you think it got?"

He shrugged. "A few feet, at least. More, I'm sure, where it collected in snowdrifts."

Ellen was concerned. "Too deep for us to get out of here?"

"Hell no," said John. "I don't care how deep it is, we're getting off this goddamn mountain today."

She nodded with conviction. "Okay."

19

The following weeks were surreal. After a day of hiking down the mountain, John and Ellen had made it to Nick's vehicle. That did them no good, however, as the key was lost with Nick. They continued on, walking down the road that had brought them there. Eventually, the phone signal was good enough for Ellen to call 911 for rescue.

They were treated at the hospital, where they were hydrated, nourished, and checked for frostbite or any other physical damage. There was superficial frostbite on their noses, fingers, and toes, which left them with permanent but minor skin damage. That did not upset them too badly; it was a small price to pay to be alive and safe. After treatment, the couple was then released to give their statements to the police.

In order to verify the Hunters' story and clear them of any wrongdoing, the authorities excavated the mine to search for the bodies of Nick and Nancy Sanders. After extensive efforts, they found the remains of the couple.

They also found some bodies of the creatures.

Just as the Hunters described, the animals were nightmarish. They had lean bodies covered in bristly fur, large subterranean eyes, long fangs, and strong claws. Their average size was only about two feet in length, but as pack predators they would be deadly. They were a terrifying discovery.

From a scientific standpoint, however, they were magnificent and fascinating. Especially the larger one. Being covered in hair, they were clearly some type of mammal, but unlike any ever seen before. They looked like a cross between a rodent, a marsupial, and a primate, but with no tail and no ears. And with oversized jaws full of sturdy teeth meant for shredding. They could've been part of either the Mustelidae, Aplodontia, or

Hominidae family. It would take some tests to determine which.

Cryptozoologists thought the creatures to be related to the Sasquatch and the Yeti. It was a new facet to that lore, which launched further wonder. What other creatures exist in this world that had yet to be seen?

For John and Ellen, life slowly returned to normal. They had to endure weeks of nightmares and battle depression, but everything got a little better each week. They also had to deal with the relentless reporters and photographers. Wanting their lives to be private, the couple shunned the media. They did, however, appear on a few television interviews, coaxed by the generous payment offers.

As with anything, the public's attention eventually floated on to other things. John and Ellen were left alone for the most part. Life moved on and the couple moved on with it. Their lives returned to normal.

Except now, anytime John wanted to pester Ellen or give her a hard time, he would ask her if she would like to go skiing.

And, every time, she would smirk and flip him her middle finger.

AUTHOR'S NOTE

The Mine is a novella birthed from one of my previous short stories *The Tunnel,* from my compilation book *Fragments And Shards* (2013). *The Tunnel* was received well, although some reviewers wished to know what happened after the cliffhanger ending. So… here we are. I hope readers enjoy this new version of the tale.

I want to thank my editor-in-law, Joyce Van Every, for her diligent eye and critical input.

As always, I want to thank my readers from the bottom of my heart. Without you, I would not be able to keep doing what I do.

Be safe, be kind, and be well.

ABOUT THE AUTHOR

Michael Yowell was born in Colorado, where he grew up loving horror in various forms—comics, movies, and ultimately books. He began writing short stories, some of which have now been published in various anthologies and ezines, as well as in his own books *Fragments And Shards* and *Fragments And Shards II*. His other novels include *Devilhouse*, *The Camera Eye*, *The Dogcatcher*, *The Dogcatcher II: Chupacabras*, *The Dogcatcher III: Werewolf Queen*, *Sliggers*, *Sligger Island*, *Sligger Invasion*, *Ghostfield*, *Pirantulas*, *A Touch Of Death*, and his Western *Red Pines*. He now resides in South Carolina with his wife Vanessa, where he continues to write his nightmarish tales. He can be reached at michaelyowellhorror@gmail.com.

Check out other great

Cryptid Novels!

J.H. Moncrieff

RETURN TO DYATLOV PASS

In 1959, nine Russian students set off on a skiing expedition in the Ural Mountains. Their mutilated bodies were discovered weeks later. Their bizarre and unexplained deaths are one of the most enduring true mysteries of our time. Nearly sixty years later, podcast host Nat McPherson ventures into the same mountains with her team, determined to finally solve the mystery of the Dyatlov Pass incident. Her plans are thwarted on the first night, when two trackers from her group are brutally slaughtered. The team's guide, a superstitious man from a neighboring village, blames the killings on yetis, but no one believes him. As members of Nat's team die one by one, she must figure out if there's a murderer in their midst—or something even worse—before history repeats itself and her group becomes another casualty of the infamous Dead Mountain.

Gerry Griffiths

CRYPTID ZOO

As a child, rare and unusual animals, especially cryptid creatures, always fascinated Carter Wilde. Now that he's an eccentric billionaire and runs the largest conglomerate of high-tech companies all over the world, he can finally achieve his wildest dream of building the most incredible theme park ever conceived on the planet... CRYPTID ZOO. Even though there have been apparent problems with the project, Wilde still decides to send some of his marketing employees and their families on a forced vacation to assess the theme park in preparation for Opening Day. Nick Wells and his family are some of those chosen and are about to embark on what will become the most terror-filled weekend of their lives—praying they survive. STEP RIGHT UP AND GET YOUR FREE PASS... TO CRYPTID ZOO

Check out other great

Cryptid Novels!

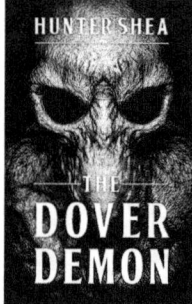

Hunter Shea

THE DOVER DEMON

The Dover Demon is real...and it has returned. In 1977, Sam Brogna and his friends came upon a terrifying, alien creature on a deserted country road. What they witnessed was so bizarre, so chilling, they swore their silence. But their lives were changed forever. Decades later, the town of Dover has been hit by a massive blizzard. Sam's son, Nicky, is drawn to search for the infamous cryptid, only to disappear into the bowels of a secret underground lair. The Dover Demon is far deadlier than anyone could have believed. And there are many of them. Can Sam and his reunited friends rescue Nicky and battle a race of creatures so powerful, so sinister, that history itself has been shaped by their secretive presence? "THE DOVER DEMON is Shea's most delightful and insidiously terrifying monster yet." – Shotgun Logic Reviews "An excellent horror novel and a strong standout in the UFO and cryptid subgenres." –Hellnotes "Non-stop action awaits those brave enough to dive into the small town of Dover, and if you're lucky, you won't see the Demon himself!" – The Scary Reviews PRAISE FOR SWAMP MONSTER MASSACRE "B-horror movie fans rejoice, Hunter Shea is here to bring you the ultimate tale of terror!" – Horror Novel Reviews "A nonstop thrill ride! I couldn't put this book down." – Cedar Hollow Horror Reviews

Armand Rosamilia

THE BEAST

The end of summer, 1986. With only a few days left until the new school year, twins Jeremy and Jack Schaffer are on very different paths. Jeremy is the geek, playing Dungeons & Dragons with friends Kathleen and Randy, while Jack is the jock, getting into trouble with his buddies. And then everything changes when neighbor Mister Higgins is killed by a wild animal in his yard. Was it a bear? There's something big lurking in the woods behind their New Jersey home. Will the police be able to solve the murder before more Middletown residents are ripped apart?